My Life
With Lukas

(On Topanga Canyon Boulevard)

BEST KID EVER

Eric A. Walters

This is a work of fiction. All of the characters, organizations, and events portrayed in this book are either products of the author's imagination or are used fictitiously.

While every precaution has been taken in the preparation of this book, the author and/or publisher assumed no responsibility for errors or omissions, or for damages resulting from the use of the information contained within.

My Life with Lukas (On Topanga Canyon Boulevard): Best Kid Ever. First Edition.

ISBN-13: 978-1-7325853-2-4

Edited by Katie Naum

FROM THE AUTHOR

Writing is a curious thing. The inspiration for this book, along with my previous books, comes from a series of short stories I wrote for a flash fiction class at UCLA. I was also looking for a unique way to share the many photos I had taken during trips to Southern California and Switzerland. *My Life with Lukas (On Topanga Canyon Boulevard)* was born during a drive along Topanga Canyon Boulevard.

I had always imagined Lukas' arrival to be at the beginning of his freshman year. But in reflecting on the stories I wanted to tell and the timeline of those stories, it made more sense to have Lukas arrive in the middle of his sophomore year.

Such is the consequence of being an amateur writer and having an active mind focused on an evolving story.

WHAT'S NORMAL?

ONE

It seemed hard to believe that Lukas had just graduated Malibu High. Considering the circumstances that brought him here and kept him here, he had finished his high school career on a high note. I was extremely proud of him. He had worked hard, made All County in soccer and starred in the lead of the Malibu Players version of *High School Musical*. Although he never made the National Honor Society nor did he ever achieve straight As, he was well-adjusted, bright, inquisitive, and sensible. Most important of all, he had maintained his sarcasm and his sense of humor through it all.

He had inspired me as well. Thanks to his support— and constant nagging—I'd self-published my first book, *My Life with Lukas (On Topanga Canyon Boulevard)*. I never could have imagined that, when Lukas accidentally left a copy at the Barnes & Noble in Topanga, someone in the publishing community would have found it "an interesting read." I credited my success to being the unlikeliest of authors: a high school physics teacher who wrote the story of his young cousin coming to live with him. I was never quite sure the book was any good, but knowing that Lukas had read the entire thing and given it "two enthusiastic thumbs up" was reward enough for me.

I was surprised when I received a phone call from the manager of the Barnes & Noble at the Grove in Los Angeles, telling me that my book had been found at a sister store (Lukas had slipped one and asking me if I'd like to join their Emerging Authors Reading Program. Even with a published book, I was still extremely reticent about sharing my work. It had taken me weeks to share it with my dad or with Lukas. Laying out my life story for everyone to read was a challenge; laying out my emotional attachment to that story was even more daunting.

The reading was to be held in a large area on the second floor near the registers. I noticed indentations on the floor when I arrived there, which suggested that the store's employees had moved the displays of children's toys and games to another area. Approximately fifty folding chairs had been set up. A small table stood next to the podium, piled with new copies of my book.

Lukas came bounding up to me with a coffee in his hand. He wore his usual outfit: a T-shirt (today's version featured a weird-looking robot apparently called Voltron), baggy khaki shorts, and black Converse sneakers. I wore pressed khaki pants and a dark blue polo shirt. We were like the *Odd Couple* meets *The Fosters*.

His unbridled energy suggested he had quite a few espresso shots in that cup. "Nervous?" he asked me, nearly bouncing up and down from excitement.

I pointed out to the fifty empty chairs.

"There's no one here," I noted.

"You'll have a big crowd soon enough," he reassured me. He was always a source of optimism.

I couldn't help but quote my favorite line from the *Odd Couple*. "Crowd? You couldn't get a good checker game going here."

An elderly lady walked off the escalator. She looked around and her eyes settled on the stack of books. She approached me slowly.

"Is this the book reading?" she asked

"Yes," I answered. I picked up a copy of my book and held it out to her. "I'd be happy to sign a copy for you."

"*My Life with Lukas*? This isn't the reading with Danielle Steele?" She sounded disappointed. So was I.

"No, it's not." *Great*, I thought. Not only did I have no attendees, I was up against Danielle Steele. Emerging author versus *New York Times* bestseller.

"But his book is awesome," Lukas interjected. "'Cuz he's my dad and he wrote it." It took him a while, but

Lukas eventually started calling me "dad." It was a small thing, but it spoke volumes.

The elderly lady rolled her eyes and called over a store employee to inquire about the Danielle Steele reading. It turned out she was there a week early.

"You could always stay for my reading," I suggested hopefully.

She must have forgotten to have her prune juice that morning. She looked at the cover of my book and announced, "I don't want to hear that crap," before hobbling off. She may as well have taken my book and beaten it with her cane.

Lukas gave me a hug. "Even if no one shows up, I'm still proud of you."

I felt like I was going to throw up. I told Lukas I was going to the bathroom. He said he'd go find some attendees.

It was 10 AM on a Saturday morning. I looked out the window. The Grove was entirely deserted. "Where are you going to find anyone now?"

"Dude, don't worry. You go to the bathroom. I'll go find some peeps."

I went into the restroom and splashed some water on my face, taking a moment to gather my courage. When I walked back out to the floor, I was pleased to see a group of friendly faces seated in the front row. There was my colleague and office mate, Dr. Patricia Branigan; my dad Matt, a former Los Angeles Police Commissioner; and Lukas' best buddy Emery. Pat apologized for being late. As usual, there was traffic on the 10.

My dad looked around at the empty chairs. "Sparse crowd," he noted. I was happy with even three supporters.

Then, like the Pied Piper of Hamlin, Lukas rode triumphantly up the escalator, followed by a crowd of forty people.

I gaped in shock before pulling Lukas aside as he directed the large group of Japanese tourists he'd managed to wrangle into the store to their seats. "Where did you find them?" I asked.

They'd been at the nearby Farmers Market as part of a tour of the United States. Lukas had lured them over by telling them that a famous American author would be doing a reading from his latest book and signing copies.

I was curious. "Do they even speak English?"

Lukas laughed. "Think about it, dude. You'll have an international audience."

Lukas was the only person I knew who could pull off a stunt like this. I would have been too nervous to attempt it.

The buzz from the tourists generated excitement throughout the store. Several other patrons arrived, picking up a copy of my book and flipping through it. They quickly found a seat, apparently eager to hear me read. Lukas snapped a picture of the huge crowd.

It was standing room only by the time the store manager had introduced me. I was so nervous that I barely heard a word he said. As I started to read, I looked in the back and saw Lukas beaming. He gave me a thumb's up. I smiled back and started.

"Will Rogers State Beach was oddly quiet for the last day of summer vacation. As a teacher, I loved June, July, and August. After a long school year filled with grading papers, planning lessons, and endless meetings, summer offered me time to reflect on my accomplishments over the past year and do some interesting professional development—as well as generally procrastinate about finishing a second script for my TV series."

I skipped ahead several pages.

"The Top of Topanga was oddly quiet for the last day of summer vacation. As a seventeen-year-old, Lukas loved summer vacation. After a long school year filled with detentions, missed homework assignments, and soccer practice, summer offered Lukas time to hang at the beach with his friends, skateboard along the

Santa Monica Pier and generally ignore the stresses of being a 'troubled' teenager at Malibu High School."

I took a breath. Lukas screamed, "That is my dad!"

I beamed with pride. "And that is the best kid ever."

TWO

Even though it was the first day of Christmas vacation, I was up as usual by 6 AM. I went for a run and stopped on the way home for a coffee at the Calabasas Coffee Bean + Tea Leaf.

I had mixed feelings about being on vacation. I actually missed my students and being at school, and usually found a way to fill my free time with schoolwork. My favorite thing about any vacation, though, was watching reruns of Perry Mason. Once I got back home, I immediately turned on the TV and settled in.

"That question is incompetent, irrelevant, and immaterial," Hamilton Burger proclaimed—a line that was required to be in every episode.

And here came the Perry Mason retort: "I disagree, your honor. The question is quite relevant."

True to form, Hamilton Burger slumped down in his chair with that "Oh crap, not again" look on his face. I wondered if he got tired of losing to Perry and why he didn't assign another assistant district attorney to a Perry Mason case.

My studio apartment was a model of organization and neatness. Magazines were stacked on the coffee table in the order in which I received them. The books on the shelf next to the sofa were arranged in subject order, and then in alphabetical order. If I failed as a teacher, I could have a job as a sales associate at the local bookstore. Even the condiments in my refrigerator were arranged alphabetically.

I liked order in my life. I tended the follow the same schedule every day, traveling the same route to and from school, parking in the same space at the local shopping center. Disruptions to my daily schedule and routine were simply inconveniences that prevented me from getting my work done. I liked routine. I liked the routine of my life.

I finished my coffee, placed the paper cup in the recycling bin and picked up a pile of physics exam papers and blue booklets. I was ready to grade! Then the doorbell rang.

"It's open," I yelled. My dad shuffled on in.

"Grandpa Matt," as he was affectionately known by everyone, was an older man of about sixty-five, wearing golf shorts, a Lacoste polo and New Balance sneakers. All of his time playing golf during his retirement had given his skin a bronze glow. He greeted me with his usual brevity. "Hey, Noah."

"Dad, what are you doing here?" Now that he was retired, he had a lot of free time to show up unannounced.

"First day of Christmas vacation. Thought I'd surprise you by taking you out to breakfast," he offered.

I was prepared for the quick parental retort. "That's nice of you. But I've got about forty exams to grade."

"You shouldn't be working so early. Especially on vacation."

"These exams aren't going to grade themselves." I never won the school-life balance argument, but I always felt compelled to try regardless.

Dad poured himself a cup of coffee, the first of many to come. Even when he was in the Los Angeles Police Department, he was known as the Coffee Commissioner.

"So, how was the date last night," he said without any preamble.

There was nothing worse than having your dad oversee your social life, and yet, here I was. Dad had set me up with a woman in his professional network. I knew he was going to be pained to hear that I had cancelled once again. He'd spent a lot of time and energy getting this Sgt. Peters to go out with me. The guilt trip would soon follow. I decided to get it over with.

"Aren't you tired of being alone?" he asked in response.

"I'm not alone. I have my kids, school," I gestured awkwardly, "...you know." *Such a lame excuse*, I thought.

"That's not living. You're losing your life to your job." This certainly wasn't the first time I'd heard *that* statement.

I knew he was right, but I wasn't going to give him the satisfaction of knowing it. He certainly didn't lead by example. He'd worked sixteen-hour days as police commissioner. The only time we'd see him was on TV.

"And isn't that what you did?" I asked.

Then came his usual retort. "We're not talking about me. Promise me, you'll call her and at least apologize."

I acquiesced. It was the least I could do.

"You know, you're not getting any younger," he added. "Your mom would want to see you happy."

Pulling the Mom card added a new level of guilt.

"I am happy," I said defensively. "I'm happy with my life just the way it is."

It seemed clear this argument would end in a tie, so my dad gave up. "I'll leave you to your grading," he said. "Maybe when you're done, we can grab lunch."

And with that, he placed his coffee cup in the dishwasher, shook my hand, and left. I grabbed a stack of papers and started counting them. Again. The pile never seemed to get any smaller.

There was a knock on the door.

"I'm still going to be grading, Dad!" I called out, annoyed.

I looked up to see my older cousin Lisa standing at the door. She was impeccably dressed as usual, with her media credentials hung around her neck. I often thought she did that on purpose, to remind me that I was 'just a teacher,' while she was an internationally-known investigative reporter for CBN. Sometimes I wondered if she even went about her daily life with a microphone, always ready to report a breaking story.

Despite this mild resentment, Lisa and I had always been close. Ever since I was an only child, Lisa always felt more like a sister than a cousin to me. We grew up one street apart in Encino, went to the same private school, and spent much of our free time together. Whenever I had a problem, Lisa was the first person I talked to. She helped me through some difficult teenage times and I helped her as well. She was much more extroverted than I was, but one of the many things I loved about her was that she never faulted me for that. My colleagues often assumed my introverted nature meant I was always uninterested. It wasn't that I was uninterested; I was just more reflective. Lisa knew me better, though—and also knew that every time she called, I was too busy with school to spend time with family. While we remained fast friends, our paths in life had diverged over the past few years.

"Hey! What is this? Family day in Calabasas?" I laughed. "My dad was just here."

"Yeah, I just saw him outside!" she said, before going on and on about some big story that had brought her to Los Angeles.

I listened, surprised that she made a detour up here to Calabasas. The only stories we had here were celebrity sightings, like a teen pop sensation allegedly throwing eggs at a neighbor's house.

Lisa placed her briefcase at the end of the sofa and sat down. She surveyed my studio apartment. "Neat as usual," she commented.

I sat on the arm of the sofa. This second intrusion into my grading bothered me. Even if it was family.

"So why are you here? What do you want?" I suppose I sounded a little snotty and aggravated.

"Why do you think I want something?" she retorted.

"Because you only call when you want something. And since you're here in person, you must really want something." I was very good at seeing right through her. She could see right through me as well, though.

And then came the windup. "I do have something to ask you. But I'm not sure how you're going to react."

I felt my stomach start to churn. This was not going to be good.

"Out with it. If you need a favor, I'll do my best to help."

And here was the pitch. "Do you think you could take care of Lukas for a while?"

Lukas Whitmore was a typical teenager. He sat in the living room of the Whitmore family home in Miami, holding a video game controller, solely focused on beating his best friend Max.

School was often not a top priority for Lukas. His teachers said he had "learning issues," although no one could ever explain what they were. Lukas didn't have learning issues, he was just confused by what was going on and, as a result, he didn't care. He often found himself getting in trouble for 'stupid stuff.'

His focus on fashion was limited, as he was most comfortable in khaki shorts, a T-shirt and black Converse sneakers. He was often mistaken for Timothée Chalamet, with a similar slim build and tousled hair. However, Lukas did not have similar, forward-thinking career aspirations.

Max sat next to him on the sofa. He was even more of a slacker than Lukas, but also a talented gamer who had no trouble defeating his friend. "Smoked you again," he announced with satisfaction before putting the video controller down on the table. That win streak had lasted for months.

"I'll beat you sometime," Lukas grumbled.

"Never will I cede victory." Max had an odd way of constructing language.

Lukas rolled his eyes. "You are one weird dude." He got up and turned off the game console. Regular programming returned to the TV.

"We finally made it to the first day of vacation, dude."

"No school for two weeks." Lukas often struggled with the regular routine of school—both the academics and the challenges of dealing with the administration. He was always thrilled when he got to get away from it all for a while. Really though, it just meant he'd find ways to get into trouble outside of school.

"What are you doing for Christmas? Spending it with your dad?"

Lukas picked up a soccer ball off the floor and idly started bouncing it off of his knee, a nervous habit. "Nope. Dad's off in Paris on business. Or somewhere. Who knows. Who cares."

"And your mom?" Max had a little crush on Lukas' mom.

"Off in California, I think."

"You're all alone again for Christmas? Who's going to fill your stocking?" There was that funny way Max had of talking again.

"Maybe the maid. Or I'll fill it myself." It really didn't matter to Lukas. It always felt like he got coal.

"You could always hang at my house," Max offered. "It'll just be me and my parents and my sister. Besides, for some reason, they like you."

Lukas delivered a quick blow to Max's arm. "That's your family, not mine," he said. "My family is just three people who co-exist in the same house, if that.'

"Oh hey!" Max exclaimed suddenly, pointing to the TV. There Lisa was, reporting on a story from Los Angeles.

Lukas was too used to seeing his mom on TV for it to make any impression. "Yep, California. Told you so." He picked the ball back up and started bouncing it higher and higher. The final bounce was so strong that it hit the ceiling, making another small crack. You could measure Lukas' frustration by the number of cracks in the ceiling.

"You never know, maybe she'll make it home for Christmas," Max suggested, always hopeful.

Lukas was skeptical. "Doubt it. I already found the Christmas envelopes hidden in the closet."

"Gift cards again?"

"Once again." Lukas was used to the lack of thought that his parents put into gift giving. *I'd even be happy with a thoughtful card*, he thought, growing sad.

Max gave his buddy a hug. "Dude, you're losing your life to a solitary existence."

THREE

I was so surprised by Lisa's request that I knocked my pile of exams onto the floor. "Say that again?" was all I could muster in response.

"I was wondering ... if you would take care of Lukas for a while."

I'd see Lukas every year at some family event. He was a good kid – happy-go-lucky, yet sarcastic. "What, for like the rest of Christmas vacation?" I asked, confused.

Lisa laughed. "*Like.* You spend way too much time with your students. I was thinking maybe, *like*," she hesitated, "for the semester."

The whole semester? Was she crazy? I bent down to pick up the exam papers, trying to restore order.

Lisa began to make her case as I did so. She admitted that it was a lot to ask. However, she would be on assignment for the next few months, and her husband Miles needed to be in the Paris office over the same period. They didn't feel comfortable leaving Lukas by himself for that long.

She also knew that I didn't have much of a life and so did I. "From what your dad tells me, school is your life." She reframed this quickly. "You're with kids all day. Seems like you'd be a natural."

I tried to be diplomatic. "You basically ignored Lukas for years and only now are you worried about him fending for himself?"

She didn't appreciate the verbal attack. "That's not fair and you know it."

"You put your career first. You both did."

"As did you." She was right about that.

"Well, at any rate, my apartment is just too small for two people," I said, looking around. I thought that might do the trick.

She was prepared for that too, though, and offered me her summer home in Topanga. It was an awesome house—modern, grey, all steel and glass. It was the kind of house I imagined living in if I ever became successful as a television writer. I'd never be able to afford it on a teacher's salary.

She was serious. Dead serious.

Lisa never made offers blindly. She continued her argument, "Lukas could go to Malibu High with you. You could keep an eye on him. He needs it." She believed I could give him that kind of guidance. I'd worked with many academically-challenged and authority-challenged students in my career. Lukas was different, though. He was family.

"Does he know about this yet?" I had a sneaking suspicion he didn't.

"Not yet," she said briskly. "Miles and I will talk to him when I'm back in Miami."

"He might not like the idea. You're asking him to move across country to live with someone he doesn't know."

"He'll look at this as an adventure." (That would turn out to be the understatement of the century.) "Besides, I think you two would be perfect for one another," she added. I hoped she was right.

I knew I couldn't say no. After all, he was family. "All right, I'll do it," I agreed. My quiet, solitary life was soon to be upended. Maybe this new arrangement would bring a little excitement into it.

Lisa arrived back in Miami the next day. She found Lukas in his bedroom. "Knock, knock," she said in a chipper voice.

Lukas was surprised to see his mom at the door, and felt a little embarrassed. His bedroom was a mess. Clothes were piled on the floor near the dresser while the laundry basket next to it remained empty. A skateboard, soccer ball, and soccer kit were at the base of the bed. A guitar leaned against the nightstand.

"What are you doing home?" he asked, bewildered. "I saw you on TV yesterday in California."

Lisa leaned against the wall. She'd taken the red eye and felt a wave of exhaustion hit her. "I had to come home for a production meeting," she said.

Tension knotted up in Lukas' shoulders. "And not to see me?"

"Of *course* I wanted to see you," she replied, as if automatically.

"Funny that I wasn't at the top of the list."

Lisa yawned. "I'm sorry. It's just the jet lag."

"Uh huh." Lukas didn't really believe her. And he didn't really care either, he thought.

"I saw your first semester report card," she said, changing the subject. "You did pretty well. I'm proud of you."

"I'm proud of myself. That's all that matters," Lukas said, pulling back into himself and looking away.

Lisa sat down at the end of the bed. "We need to have a little talk."

Lukas laughed. "I've been behaving myself," he said, rolling his eyes.

"I know. This is something more serious."

"Go on." Lukas frowned. He hated these 'serious talks.' They were never good news.

"You know that your dad will need to be in Paris for the next six months. And I'm going to be on assignment for a while as well."

"You told me before you left." Lukas really needed a calendar for when his parents were actually home. "So what's your solution?" He figured it would be a full-time nanny or something ridiculous like that.

"I've talked to your cousin Noah. What would you think about living with him for the semester?"

"In California?" To Lukas, that seemed like another planet.

"Yes, in California."

Lukas sat at full attention. "But what about my friends? And Max? And all my stuff here?" He started to shake. This felt like the greatest parental abandonment of all time.

Lisa tried to reassure him. "You'll only be away until May. You'll make new friends out there and you'll have your old friends here when you get back. You like Noah, right?"

"He's a teacher. A little square, I don't know." Lukas laughed at the irony. The misfit student being placed with the rule-following teacher.

"Maybe he'll keep you in check."

You certainly haven't, Lukas thought. Just then Lisa's cell phone rang. She answered it and scampered out of the room without saying another word to Lukas.

"That's mingin'." Lukas was known to invoke obscure Scottish sayings when he was frustrated. He picked up his game controller and threw it against the wall in anger, watching it shatter into a thousand or so pieces.

I drove up through the Santa Monica Mountains and finally found Lisa's house. The sign outside read 19 Emmerdale Trail. It wasn't exactly as I remembered it, but it was thoughtfully-designed, very Southern California. A porch wrapped around the front of the house, providing an expansive view of the valley and the Pacific. This was now my home.

As I got out of my car (my pride and joy, a black Audi A6) and looked out over the canyon, the loud rattle of a U-Haul truck soon disrupted the peace and quiet of Emmerdale Trail. I looked over to see my dad struggling to pull the truck into the driveway; he came dangerously close to veering off into the canyon.

The truck rumbled to a stop and Matt hopped out. He was clearly agitated. "Criminey dutch. These roads are crazy." I couldn't help but laugh when he used antiquated phrases like that.

We started pulling boxes out of the U-Haul. I unlocked the door and was hit with the staleness of a house that hadn't been lived in for years. I placed my box on the floor and slid open the glass door. Fresh air flooded into the room. I stepped out on the porch. The view was incredible.

"This is going to be a big change for you," my dad said. He was right.

"You mean living in Topanga?"

"No. Taking care of a kid. Who's not a student."

That responsibility would turn out to be an awesome one.

FOUR

Topanga was a whole new world. I'd said goodbye to Ralph's in Calabasas, my local Coffee Bean, and my eternal dream of seeing a Kardashian or Justin Bieber at Walgreens. Now I would dine regularly at the Canyon Diner, get my coffee at Malibu Coffee + Tea, and shop at the Topanga Market.

The morning sunlight was glistening on the Pacific Ocean as I sat in a blue funky chair inside Malibu Coffee + Tea. I'd just registered Lukas for the spring semester at Malibu High. My explanation to Cynthia, the school secretary, was so convoluted that I'm not sure if she or I understood it. But since I was Mr. Whitmore, the trusted physics teacher, Cynthia processed the paperwork without question and without complaining.

I looked at the very thick folder in front of me and rubbed my fingers over the label: *Lukas Whitmore, Permanent Record.* During his short time in high school, Lukas had accumulated a laundry list of violations: late to class, no hall pass, late to school, disrespect to the teacher. To me, though, it seemed pretty clear that he wasn't a bad kid—he just got into trouble for a lot of little things that built up over time. The next six months were either going to be fun or a challenge. I hoped for fun but feared a challenge.

"Can I join you?" I looked up to see Dr. Pat Branigan standing before me. She wore running tights and a Malibu High School T-shirt and she had a water bottle in her hand, fresh from a run. Pat was the school psychologist at Malibu High; as a result of a ceiling collapse ten years ago, she and I ended up sharing an office. We'd been good friends ever since.

"Isn't this a little out of your neighborhood?" she asked me. "Long drive just for coffee."

I laughed. "Short drive now. I've moved to Topanga."

Pat slid into the chair across from me. "What prompted that?"

I pointed to the thick folder on the table.

Pat spun it around and looked at the cover. "Lukas Whitmore? Relative of yours?"

"That, Pat, is my cousin."

"And you have his permanent record ... why?"

"Guess who's going to be living with me the next six months." Based on the *Friends*-style quip a moment before, I half-expected a TV show spit-take.

"Lukas?"

"Seriously," I replied, feeling at a loss for words. I couldn't admit I had a sinking feeling that I was probably in over my head.

"How'd this all come about?" Pat was a talented psychologist. She was very effective at probing a client's motivations.

I recounted how Lisa had come to Calabasas, begging me to watch Lukas for the semester.

"I dare say that's quite a request and quite a commitment." She was right, of course, but given the circumstances, it was the right thing to do.

Dr. Pat flipped through the file, taking it all in. She chuckled. "He's like the anti-you," she joked.

I was definitely going to need her professional advice, but she didn't seem too worried on my behalf. "Well he'll be in good hands, Mr. Champion of the Marginalized," she said playfully before standing to leave. She was half-serious: she knew that if there was a kid on the boundary, I was there to champion them. Maybe it was because I wished someone had championed me when I was struggling.

Max watched from a chair as Lukas sat on his bed, tossing a soccer ball in the air. "Dude, I can't believe you're moving to California," he said at last.

Lukas was still in shock, but acted nonchalant. "Believe it, dude. By this time next week, I'll be soaking up the rays in Malibu."

"You seem pretty cool about the whole thing."

"Well, one, I don't have a choice. And two, my parents don't seem to want me here. So, three, I may as well make the best of it." The soccer ball flew higher and higher.

"What do you think school is like out there?" Max had set Lukas up for a witty, sarcastic retort.

"Oh, probably the same as here. Classrooms. Teachers. Books. Why would you think it's any different?"

Max was good at playing innocent. "I was just asking."

Lukas rolled his eyes. "I'm sure I'll get in trouble out there too."

"And don't forget the California girls."

"Yep, California girls."

Lukas picked up his phone and sat on the chair behind Max, raising it up for a selfie.

FIVE

After Max went home, Lukas sat at the top of the stairs, listening as his parents spoke quietly in the living room below. After many years of eavesdropping, he knew it was just the right spot to not only see the action but to hear it as well.

Lukas was surprised that his father Miles had come home right after Christmas. He'd hadn't expected to see his dad for a while. Lukas didn't know what they were about to discuss, but couldn't think of anything bigger than his transfer to California.

Miles was always direct. "Are we sure this is the best thing for Lukas?"

"Well, Noah has already registered him at school, so…" Lisa sighed. "Besides, what else are we going to do with him?"

Miles nodded in agreement.

"Maybe a new start will help straighten him out," she continued.

"I don't think anything will straighten that kid out." Miles was all business, even when it came to family.

Lisa chuckled. "Had I known how much trouble he would be, I might have reconsidered having a kid."

That line hit Lukas hard. He bolted upright and tried to catch his breath. There was a big difference between not being wanted now and not being wanted in the first place. All he had ever wanted was to be wanted.

Lukas dropped his phone and ran down the stairs, but when he reached his parents, he didn't even know where to begin. "Is that what I am to you—trouble?" he blurted out.

Lisa and Miles were surprised to see him.

"Lukas, I thought you were packing," Miles commented.

"I'm done. I'm so done," he replied, furious. He turned to his dad. "And you, I'm just 'that kid' to you?"

Miles' face dropped. "I didn't mean it that way," he said, clearly uncomfortable.

Lukas grew more and more angry. "How many other ways can you mean it? All I ever wanted to know is that I mattered to the two of you."

Miles tried to calm the situation to no avail. "You do matter."

"And how do I matter? I get no love. I get no respect."

"We respect you," Miles insisted.

Lukas took a deep breath, trying to calm down, and lowered his voice. "Love is more than just a big house. A big house with just me in it." He pointed at his parents. "Not you. And not you. Just me."

Lisa tried to defend their position. "You know well and good that we work hard to put this roof over your head."

Lukas grew even quieter. "You don't get it, do you? I guess I'd rather live 3000 miles away with someone I barely know than stay here with people who wish I was never born."

With that, Lukas turned and ran back upstairs. He quickly grabbed his duffel bag, backpack and skateboard, and returned back downstairs with them. Lisa was alarmed. "Where do you think you're going?" she cried.

"I'm out of here," Lukas announced. "If you don't want me here, I'm not staying."

Miles attempted to block his path. "You're not going anywhere, mister."

"Just try to stop me." Lukas bulldozed past him, flung open the front door and left, slamming it shut behind him.

Lisa started crying. "Miles, go after him," she said in a choked voice.

Miles groaned and looked away. "He'll be back. He always comes back," he said at last. He could not have been more wrong.

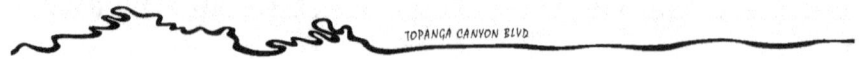

I took a step back in the room that would soon become Lukas', admiring the paint job I'd just finished, when my dad entered. Dad closed the door partway and noticed a blue handprint on the other side.

"What's with the handprint?" he asked.

I pointed to the roller pan and then to my hand. "Way to leave your mark," he said dryly.

I chuckled. "What do you think?"

"Of the handprint?" he asked. He knew I meant the room. "I don't think HGTV will be calling you any time soon," he said at last. The Whitmore sarcasm had returned. "But it's not too bad." Then he looked up at the illuminated letter J and the illuminated hashtag on the opposite wall. "Now those are corny."

"Give me some credit for trying. He can take them down if he wants. I just want him to feel welcome when he gets here."

"Hashtag blue bedroom," Dad muttered.

I ignored him, rinsing the paintbrush off in the bucket and setting it down before taking a picture of the room.

"So, can I give you any parenting advice?" Dad asked. Regardless of the situation, my dad always had a piece of advice. Whether I chose to take it or not was another story.

"From you? Father of the year."

"I was just going to suggest that you be supportive and present. You know, like being a teacher."

"Oh, like you were present after Mom died," I snapped.

Dad gave me a look. "Being police commissioner was a huge responsibility. I put food on the table for you, didn't I? We all made the best of a very bad situation."

He just doesn't get it, I thought. Maybe it was time for some real talk. I drew a deep breath. "Seeing Mom…"

Just then, my phone chirped. The newly-arrived text message completely derailed my train of thought.

"Uh oh."

"What's wrong?" Dad asked.

"Looks like Lukas flew the coop a little early."

The texts from Lisa said that Lukas had overheard a conversation between his parents and stormed out of the house. Apparently, he headed straight to the airport. He was on the next flight out of Miami. How he managed that as a minor was anybody's guess but, long story short, he'd be landing in Los Angeles in three hours.

"You better get to the airport, 'Dad,'" my dad said. He paused for a moment, considering. "Do you want me to come with you?"

I declined. I needed to be a dad by myself.

SIX

I sat in the chair at Gate 76. *These have to be the most uncomfortable seats in the world*, I thought. I wondered who would wake up in the morning and say, "I'd like to design airport seating for a living."

The waiting seemed to take forever. I looked at Lukas' picture on my phone. I looked around the gate area and saw a number of eager families waiting for the next flight to back to Miami. I stood up and nervously walked around the gate area and returned to my seat. I checked my phone again and then looked up at the digital signage. I then headed to the desk.

"Are you sure this is the flight from Miami?" I asked. I was very nervous. I told the gate agent I was waiting for my kid. It was odd to refer to Lukas as "my kid," but I didn't feel like going through the 'he's my cousin and he's staying with me' story.

The gate agent looked frustrated. "Same gate it was arriving at when you asked a half an hour ago. Same gate it was arriving at when you asked an hour ago. The plane just touched, sir. They will be deplaning in a few minutes." She probably thought I was a lunatic.

The gate door finally opened and passengers started deplaning. I looked at the picture on my phone again and then tried to match it to the passengers. No match. Even Gene Rayburn would have been disappointed in me. The line eventually slowed to a trickle. Then the pilot and copilot exited.

I approached the gate agent again. "Are you sure this is the flight from Miami? My kid still hasn't gotten off."

I thought the gate agent was going to fling the pile of luggage tags in my face. "Yes, this is the flight from Miami," she said in a strained voice. "Sometimes we have a flight attendant escort unaccompanied minors off the plane last."

At that very moment, a kid finally exited the plane, carrying his overstuffed Adidas duffel bag, backpack, and skateboard. Beats headphones hung around his neck.

The kid looked down at his phone, then at me. A big grin came over his face. He dropped his duffel bag and skateboard and ran over to me, giving me a big hug.

"Lukas!" I shouted, loud enough for the entire terminal to hear. "Welcome to California!"

Lukas wiped his hands on his pants with exaggerated disgust. "Cousin Noah. Dude, you're all sweaty. Take a shower, will you?" He looked at me and smirked. Lukas had arrived.

TOPANGA CANYON BLVD

I packed Lukas' luggage in the trunk of my car while Lukas gave the car a quick once-over. "Sweet ride, dude," he said. Something told me he would be calling me *dude* from now on.

We pulled out of the parking garage and headed to the 405. Lukas immediately started punching through all the buttons on the car stereo.

"Dude, you need a better station selection." There it was again, *dude*. He was charming, I thought. Or annoying.

Lukas contorted himself into a pretzel in the passenger seat and started air drumming on the dashboard.

"Nervous about being here?" I asked.

"Hell yeah. But not in that teenage angst, freeform drama sort of way. I'm nervous, but I'm excited." I could only hope I could sustain that excitement for him.

"And what about living with me?" I continued.

His voice changed and grew more sarcastic. "I'm sure I'll get used to it. Where else am I gonna stay?"

"I heard things ended badly for you in Miami."

"You might say that," he replied. "But I'm here now. So let's put that behind me."

I liked Lukas' positive attitude. I reminded him that this parenting thing was all new to me. Lukas reminded me that he was used to being on his own, so having an adult in his life—one who might actually care—was new to him as well. We agreed to be patient with one another.

Lukas started looking around the car like he was scavenging for food. He found a copy of one of my scripts stashed in the side compartment.

"What's this?" he asked.

I was always nervous about sharing my work. "You don't need to look at that," I replied.

Lukas was insistent. "C'mon. What is it?"

"That's a script."

Lukas became curious. "For what, like a TV show?"

I came clean. "Yes, I've been working on a show. Well, sort of."

"What's it about?"

"A high school science teacher who becomes a famous television writer."

"You should have made it about a high school science teacher who takes in his annoying cousin." Clearly, Lukas' sense of humor was very similar to mine.

"That's funny."

"But dude, that is so cool," he continued. "I wanna read it. Is that ok?"

"Let's get you settled into life out here and then you can read it."

Lukas turned and looked out the window. Each building we passed—Randy's Donuts, UCLA, In-N-Out, Getty Center—provided Lukas with an opportunity to ask, "What building is that?" He even got excited when we passed some random hotel.

It was starting to get annoying. "Are you going to ask about every building we pass?" I finally asked.

He had a witty retort ready to go. "I'm trying to be an engaged, curious student. I thought you'd appreciate that, being a teacher."

"Are you always this sarcastic?"

"Pretty much, yeah. I bet you're starting to regret this." He was quick to assume the worst. Regret was a strong word. Maybe I was starting to wonder what I'd gotten myself into.

Overall, though, he seemed like a good kid. "Actually, I think we just might get along great," I said.

Lukas turned quiet and stared out the window at the passing scenery. He eventually dozed off. He remained asleep through the Sepulveda Pass, along the 101 and up through Topanga Canyon. He'd clearly had a rough day and I wanted to give him the time and space he needed. *Yes*, I thought, *my first successful parenting decision!*

At last, we pulled into the driveway on Emmerdale Trail. The sound of the tires crunching on the pebble driveway underneath woke Lukas up.

"We're home," I announced.

Lukas looked at his watch. "Dude, that ride was like two hours." He surveyed his new home. "But sweet house." I realized that, even though his parents owned this house, Lukas might have never been here. I never even asked him if he'd ever been California before. I'd just assumed that he had.

Lukas ran up to the edge of the ravine and stared off into the distance, taking a deep breath. I was starting to understand that Lukas might be a more reflective teenager than I had originally thought. While he acclimated himself to his new surroundings, I unloaded his luggage from the car.

Lukas squinted into the distance. "Is that the Pacific Ocean?"

I came up behind him. "Yes, that's the Pacific." I pointed off into the distance. "If you look way down there, that's Santa Monica."

"Can we go to the beach?" That seemed like an odd request.

"Now?"

"Yeah, why not? What else do you have to do? I wanna see the beach." Lukas took out his phone and snapped a quick selfie of us. Apparently, he wanted to remember this moment for time immemorial.

"You've got to get settled in. You—and I—have school tomorrow."

Lukas saluted. "Yes, sir." He grabbed his duffel bag, backpack, and skateboard and we headed inside.

"I have to warn you, it's a bit messy in here!" I said as we entered the house Lukas looked around. His definition and my definition of messy were completely different.

"Dude, this is not messy. You should see my room back home."

Lukas dropped his stuff on the floor, plopped down on the sofa, kicked off his black Converse sneakers and turned on the TV.

"What channel is ESPN? And can I get a water?"

I put on my strict parenting hat. "ESPN is Channel 28. And if you want water, the refrigerator's right over there." I sounded like such a loser.

"Dude, slow your parenting roll. You're a fill-in dad, not my actual dad."

The little brat, I thought. "Fill-in or not, I'm in charge. And this is only going to work with some mutual respect and understanding."

"I didn't ask to be here," Lukas snapped.

"What happened to 'I'm excited to be here?'" I demanded, growing frustrated. Now I knew how that gate agent felt.

Lukas quickly apologized. "I'm not used to someone telling me what to do," he explained.

I knew I had to be patient, the same way I needed to be patient when a student asked a truly stupid question. "It's ok. We're going to see how this goes," I said.

"I can live with that," Lukas said.

"I'll give you the freedom to be a teenager as long as you give me the respect of being the adult in charge," I said. "Deal or no deal?"

"Deal," Lukas replied. Then he smirked. "But I have a question. Where do they put the stands when the model walks away with the briefcase?"

"Where did *that* come from?" I asked.

"Don't you ever wonder about things like that?" he replied. The kid had a curious mind. Just like me.

"Let's be serious," I said. "You buckle down, do your schoolwork, and do your best." It seemed like a reasonable plan to me. Lukas quickly agreed.

I told Lukas to grab his stuff. He'd find his room upstairs, first door on the left. "You'll need to be up early tomorrow," I reminded him. "First day of school for you!"

Lukas saluted again and bounded upstairs to his bedroom.

I took a deep breath, grabbed a bottle of water, and stepped outside, sitting down on the deck. In some ways, the world seemed so big before. Now with Lukas here, it seemed so much smaller.

"Well, that wasn't as bad as I thought it would be," I said to myself. "I think this might work out ok."

Lukas opened the door to his bedroom and fumbled around for the light. His hand landed in wet paint. In struggling to find the light switch and close the door, Lukas left his handprint just below mine.

"Already making a mess," Lukas said to himself.

He sat on the floor of his new bedroom, his back against the wall. He looked up and saw a giant J above him.

That is corny. And man, this room is really *blue*, he thought.

Lukas spotted a soccer ball on the floor and scooped it up. Standing up, he started bouncing it off his knee. He didn't think he should try to hit the ceiling.

"Well, that wasn't as bad as I thought it would be," Lukas said to himself. "I think this might work out ok.

SEVEN

This was my first official full day of dad duty. And my first official act was to awaken a sleepy teenager and bring him to a new school in a new city where he didn't know anyone. I'd gotten up extra early to get dressed and eat. Something told me getting Lukas ready for school was going to be a challenge. I only had one chance to get this right.

I slowly opened the door to his bedroom and was surprised to see Lukas sitting on the bed fully dressed. He wore an outfit similar to his arrival outfit yesterday—khaki shorts, a T-shirt and black Converse sneakers. He appeared to be visibly shaking.

"Are you ok?" It was the only question I could come up with.

"Do I look ok?" he replied.

"Well, no. You're shaking. Are you nervous?"

"Damn right I am dude. I thought this was going to be easy. But I don't know anyone here."

"You know me," I said. Even as I said it, I knew I was a teacher and didn't count.

Lukas was one of the popular kids at his school in Miami. Everyone knew him. Everyone liked him. Helping him fit in here would be my second parenting challenge—a much greater one than rousing him out of bed.

I suggested that perhaps I could introduce him to some of my students.

"Why don't you just write DORK on my forehead. Getting introduced to students by a teacher. Ugh." Lukas let out a sizable groan.

"Just be yourself," I said helplessly. My advice was getting worse.

"You're not helping," he groaned. I did notice he had stopped shaking.

I gave him a hug.

"You're Lukas Whitmore. You can do this," I said.

He smiled. "You're right. I can." Boy, did I have the magic parenting touch.

TOPANGA CANYON BLVD

The drive to Malibu High took us through the Santa Monica Mountains. Lukas was glued to his window, mesmerized by what he saw. I was impressed by how he could contort himself into various shapes in the front seat.

A chill came over me as I watched him staring out the window. For the next six months, this young man was my responsibility. It was a responsibility I would not take lightly.

We pulled into the parking lot. Lukas hopped out of the car and slung his backpack over his back. He did exemplify California-transplant cool.

I grabbed my briefcase from the back seat.

Lukas laughed. "Now who's the dork?" he teased. I let it go.

"We need to check in at the main office so you can get your class schedule and your locker info. They'll have to fingerprint you and take the required blood sample."

"Dude, what?" Lukas gasped, growing pale.

I smirked. "I'm kidding."

Lukas punched my arm. "When the Comedy Shop calls, hang up." *Another witty retort*, I thought. I snapped his picture in front of the famous Malibu Shark, but only after he had fixed his curly hair for five minutes.

We entered the school office and Cynthia, the school secretary, gave me her usual cheery hello. She looked at Lukas and asked, "And who is this young man?"

"This is my cousin Lukas. I registered him last week. Today's his first day here at Malibu."

Cynthia smiled and tapped away on her computer. Anything Cynthia did was usually accompanied by school gossip. I guess today she had none.

"Here we are. Lukas Whitmore. Oh, yes, the one with the massive permanent record." She looked up at my cousin. "You know how long it took me to scan all that in? You better not get into that kind of trouble here, mister."

Lukas blushed. "I won't," he promised.

Cynthia gave him his schedule and circled the day and his first period class, Chemistry. Lukas did a quick imitation of something blowing up.

"You ready?" I asked.

"As ready as I'll ever be."

We made a few detours on the trip to the chemistry lab. I showed Lukas my office, his locker location ("Centrally located," he noted) and the quad. Several students looked at us curiously, wondering why Mr. Whitmore was showing around a student.

We finally arrived at the chemistry lab. I opened the door and walked Lukas in, introducing him to his teacher, Ms. Hurt. I knew that Lukas struggled academically and I trusted he'd be in good hands with Ms. Hurt. We'd been science department colleagues for years; she was patient and kind, but firm. I didn't want a science class to be his academic downfall here at Malibu.

As they talked, a kid in the back yelled out, "Who's the new dude?"

I walked over to him. "That new dude is my kid. So be nice to him."

The outspoken student hung his head in shame. "I'm sorry, Mr. Whitmore."

As I turned and walked away, though, I overheard the outspoken student say, "Mr. Whitmore has a kid? When did that happen?" I'd inadvertently started a rumor that would sweep across the campus before the end of the period.

I had a full schedule of classes that morning, and before I knew it, it was lunchtime. I'd been tempted to text Lukas to ask him how things were going, but I didn't want him to think he couldn't handle things on his own. Besides, considering his track record, I knew he'd probably end up in trouble for having his phone out.

The faculty section of the quad consisted of several tables where teachers could eat while keeping an eye on the student body during lunch time. It was very clique-ish. Teachers sat with their friend groups or their department peers. We were worse than the kids. Entry into a different friend group was often hard to gain, if not impossible.

I could sit at any table. I could talk to anyone. But no matter where I sat, I was often ignored, or would struggle with making a relevant comment. Each lunch period, I listened to my peers' stories about their kids' recent adventures or accomplishments. I had never had a kid story to tell or a kid photo to share.

Pat put her tray down and sat next to me. "How's it going?" She looked around. "Which one is Lukas?"

"T-shirt, khaki shorts, Timothée Chalamet hair."

"I don't see him yet."

"I think he has lunch next period." I'd failed to memorize his schedule.

"Shouldn't you check on him? What kind of parent are you?" That felt crushing, but I knew it was said in jest.

Deep down, I thought it best for Lukas to navigate the day on his own. Maybe I'd made a mistake, but I felt he needed to learn his way around by himself.

Today's seating arrangement featured a gaggle of teachers from various departments. They were very chatty, so interjecting into the conversation would be tough. This was my big chance, though: I finally had a kid story to share.

I saw my chance. "Hey guys, did I tell you ..."

That chance disappeared in an instant. "Did you all see that memo from Principal Williams—the new due date for our semester grades?" Teacher #1 interjected.

"Now we need to turn them in a day earlier!" Teacher #2 grumbled.

I kept trying. "Hey, did you see my..." Nothing. I was dying.

Even Pat gave it a shot. "Noah's cousin..." she began, but her words were lost in cross-talk. I guess my colleagues were too wound up over the new grading deadline to hear about my new parenting role.

Teacher #3 tried to defuse the situation about the new deadline. Out came the phone. "Do you all want to see pictures of my Mary on a carousel? She is so cute."

The teachers turned their attention to Teacher #3. A steady stream of "oohs," "ahhs," and "isn't she cutes" emerged from the group.

I looked over to Pat. "I give up," I said, defeated.

Lukas had just finished his last class before lunch. Four classes in a row were too much for him. He'd tried to make friends in each class, but had been unsuccessful. The other kids were more focused on academics than on making friends with the kid from Florida. During group discussions, he sat lost and confused. He imagined Max slacking through the day back home.

At lunchtime, he wasn't particularly hungry, but found his way to the cafeteria anyway. He grabbed some water and a plate of macaroni and cheese (*This looks disgusting,* he thought) and sat at an empty picnic table on the quad.

Lukas looked around at all of the other tables and, as he sat there alone, he felt like the eyes of every other student were glued on him. He started to sweat. True to high school stereotypes, each table had one of the standard-issue high school cliques. The jocks at one table, surrounded by cheerleaders; another table with the robotics team; a third table with the drama kids; a fourth table with the weirdos. Lukas looked at his table. He was all alone. *What am I doing here?*

he wondered. It had only been one morning, but he knew that if he didn't make friends soon, he might be alone for a long time. He'd gone from the popular kid in Florida to completely marginalized in Malibu. He had been lonely in his life outside of school before. Now he knew how it felt to be lonely at school. He buried his head in his lunch and tried to ignore what was going on around him.

Lukas' solitude was interrupted when the table shook. He looked up as a tall kid wearing a Malibu High Aquatics shirt sat down across from him.

"You must be the new kid," the athlete said, extending his hand. He introduced himself as Emery Cooper, president of the National Honor Society and captain of the swim team. "How's your first day going?" he asked. Apparently, Emery had been in Lukas' English class, but Lukas had been too preoccupied with trying to understand the motivations of *Mrs. Dalloway* to notice.

"Well, I don't seem to have made many friends," Lukas said, pointing to the empty table.

"Well, you made one. That's me. Consider me your personal welcome wagon."

Lukas didn't know what a welcome wagon was. He could only assume it was a California thing.

Emery explained how he had been the new kid in the middle of last year, and had been in the same situation. Lukas relaxed a little. He told Emery that he was from Florida and was staying for the semester with his cousin, Mr. Whitmore.

"Oh, we all were wondering who Mr. Whitmore was showing around this morning. You've got the double whammy. New kid and teacher as a relative." Emery laughed.

Lukas slowly began to relax. Fortunately, Emery and Lukas were in the same math class after lunch. Emery suggested they take a selfie to immortalize their new friendship.

Lukas was happy. He had made a new friend.

I sat in my office at the end of the day, waiting for the 3 PM bell to ring. Pat was next to me, reviewing a case file, and noticed me tapping my pencil on my desk.

"You are worse than an expectant father," she remarked.

I couldn't help it, I told her—I'd been worried about Lukas all day.

"Now you're just like a father." She laughed. "You spend half your life with your heart in your mouth worrying about them."

"I was really tempted to text or call him or find him at lunch. You know, see how he's doing."

"Would you have wanted your dad hovering over you the first day of school?"

"Well, no."

Pat reminded me that one of the challenges of being a parent is knowing when to let go and knowing when to offer a helping hand. I wasn't going to learn that overnight. Still...

"There's not a crash course in parenting, is there?" I joked. *If there was, I should probably take it*, I added mentally.

"Wait a minute, where is he?" I said, checking his schedule online. He should have been here by now.

"The bell *just* rang, Noah. He's probably still finding his way to your office."

"Ok, do me a favor," I said. "When he shows up, tell him to wait for me. I have to bring these forms down to the office."

"Where else do you think he's gonna go?"

I sprinted across campus to the office. Cynthia was at her usual position behind the counter, shuffling around a massive pile of folders that almost dwarfed her. I placed the forms on the counter and apologized for turning them in late.

"I imagine you've had a lot on your mind today," she replied. Thankfully, she wasn't cranky.

"I've been hoping Lukas had a good first day. I need to get back to my office. He's supposed to meet me there after his last class."

"I don't think you'll have to go back to your office to meet him," Cynthia said, pointing behind me.

I turned around. There Lukas was, sitting on the bench, his backpack between his legs and his head down.

"What are you doing here?" I asked. This was the "bad kids bench." He'd only been here a day and he was already in trouble?

Lukas sighed before responding. "Guess who slugged a classmate."

EIGHT

The drive along Topanga Canyon Boulevard was extremely quiet. I was seething.

Lukas sat quietly in the front seat, staring out the window. "Are you going to say anything?" he asked at one point. I shook my head. We pulled into the parking lot of the Canyon Diner.

"Where are we?" Lukas asked.

"Canyon Diner. My favorite restaurant."

"See, you said something," Lukas was trying but failing to defuse the situation.

We were greeted by Olivia, the waitress/hostess. She had a hip vibe to her, with about ten earrings in each ear.

"I heard you had moved down here from Calabasas," she said by way of greeting. Gossip traveled fast in Topanga.

"And who is this young man?" she quickly added, taking Lukas in. Apparently gossip didn't travel *that* fast.

"This is my cousin, Lukas," I said. "He's going to be staying with me for the next few months."

Olivia gave Lukas a big hug and then regaled him with her life story. She'd grown up in Philadelphia, and been in every theatre production at both her high school and during her college career at Loyola Marymount. She invited Lukas to come see a show for free at the Will Geer Theatricum, where she currently worked with aspiring child actors. I think she'd already developed a crush on him. Apparently, the Chalamet-hair had that effect on people.

Lukas quietly thanked her for her offer.

"Bad day?" she asked, turning to me.

"Lukas had a rough first day of school," I said. He gave me a weak smile in response, looking for sympathy or absolution. He got none from me. I was still angry.

"Sit where you'd like," Olivia said lightly. "It's pretty quiet tonight."

We sat in the back corner, under the bug zapper. Lukas stared at the menu in front of him.

Olivia showed up quickly after we seated ourselves to take our order. "Something to drink?"

I ordered a bottle of water. "Nothing for me," Lukas said quietly. Olivia scampered off to get my bottle of water.

Finally, I broke the silence. "Look at me." Lukas seemed shocked by my directness.

"What?" he asked, an edge of defensiveness in his voice.

"Don't get snotty with me. What were you thinking? Hitting another kid?"

Lukas explained that a classmate had made a crack about me "having a kid." When I pressed him about the exact language that was used, Lukas said that it didn't matter. It really didn't; I'd heard it all before. If you didn't have a tough skin, you weren't going to make it in the teaching profession.

"I feel like I've let you down," Lukas said. He started crying.

All I'd wanted for Lukas was for him to have a positive new beginning at school. Now his first day had been marred by some stupid fight.

Lukas sensed me watching him and tried to pull himself together. "Thanks for going to bat for me with Principal Williams," he said through tears.

I smiled a little. "See, there *is* some benefit to having a relative at school. He could have suspended you or, worse, expelled you."

He laughed and wiped his eyes. "At least everyone knows who I am now." Talk about being optimistic.

"You're starting off with a great reputation," I said sarcastically.

Lukas was still crying. "Are you mad at me?"

How could I stay mad at him? This was his first day in a new school, in a new city. It had to be stressful. It was even stressful for me.

"I'm not," I said. "Everyone has a rough day now and then. Everyone has a rough start. Things happen. You just need to learn from them."

"You are such a teacher," he groaned. I couldn't help but laugh before getting serious again.

"Now, we are going to put this behind us. You'll serve your detention and that's it. Fresh start, ok?"

"Yes, sir." Lukas saluted in that goofy way he had.

Olivia returned with my water and asked if we were ready to order.

"Spaghetti and meatballs," Lukas said. I knew that was his favorite meal.

"Spaghetti and meatballs, *please*," I said, reminding him of his manners.

"Please isn't on the menu," Lukas retorted. I knew he was feeling better because the sarcasm had returned.

NINE

Lukas was slowly acclimating to life in southern California. After his fight on the first day, he'd managed to stay out of trouble, except for an occasional late to class violation. He'd become best friends with Emery, and, as a result, his circle of friends had grown infinitely larger. Everyone at school knew him; everyone at school liked him. He still struggled academically, but he took the initiative to seek out extra help when he needed it. That made me happy as a teacher.

He had also grown tired of the deep blue color in his bedroom and had repeatedly asked me if we could repaint it. I finally relented. We spent a tiring afternoon at Home Depot while Lukas dithered over every possible paint choice. He finally settled on ocean blue, to remind him of Miami.

When "Painting Saturday" finally arrived, Lukas was up early to move what little furniture there was to the center of the room. Afterward, he bounded down the stairs for a bowl of cereal.

"I'm ready to paint. Are you?" he asked. He was very excited.

"I have a lot of work to do. Maybe you should paint your room yourself." It sounded harsh, but I was just giving him a hard time. It was easy to do.

Lukas grumbled. "Dude, all you do is work and grade papers. Have some fun. Grab a paintbrush, will ya?"

There was a knock on the door.

"Can I get some help here?" my dad hollered. He had primed the walls for us earlier in the week, and now stood in the doorway struggling with a box of paintbrushes and rollers, along with three cans of the famous ocean blue paint.

"Hey!" Lukas hopped up, opening the door and giving him a hug.

"I have all your stuff. Now just help this old man, ok?" Lukas took the box from my dad's hands and then dragged the paint cans into the kitchen.

"Thanks, dude. Do you want to stay and help?" He turned and rolled his eyes at me. "This one says he has too much work to do."

My dad laughed. "That's always his excuse."

Lukas took the paint cans and disappeared upstairs.

"You're not going to let him paint by himself, are you?" Dad asked, raising an eyebrow.

"Of course not, I was just giving him a hard time," I said. *It's not like he'll be doing heart surgery*, I thought.

Dad pointed at the two bowls of the cereal on the kitchen table; I knew he was thinking about the relationship between Lukas and I. "How's it going so far?" he asked.

I considered how to respond. Lukas was definitely keeping me busy. Being a "dad" was much more difficult than I thought.

"I like having someone to look after," I said finally. I knew I could be honest about that.

"I think he likes you looking after him," Dad said.

"I'm not sure why. I'm just a fill-in. Wait, what did he say to you?"

My dad sat down at the table. "He's called me a couple of times. Not to complain. He likes your parenting style." A man of few words, as usual—but kind ones. I appreciated it.

"I didn't even know I had a style," I joked.

He looked at his watch. "Let me get out of here. I have a police department luncheon to get to. You go up there and help the kid paint."

TOPANGA CANYON BLVD

I walked into Lukas' bedroom. He already had a can of paint open, filling one of the paint trays, and seemed pleased to see me. "So, you *are* going to help?"

I looked at the two hand prints on the back of the door. They reminded me of the two cereal bowls downstairs. "Let's not paint over the hands on the door, ok?" I asked suddenly.

"I wouldn't even dare," he replied. Sentimental Lukas had emerged.

I thought Lukas would have music blaring. He usually played it so loud that at times the whole house would shake. I was often surprised that our neighbors didn't call the police and file a noise complaint. Instead, the painting party turned out to be an unusually quiet affair.

"Can I ask you a question? A personal question?" he said at one point. He sounded serious.

"Depends on what it is." I didn't really like responding to personal questions, even if it was family.

"Not as a teacher," he clarified, "but as my dad, or whatever you wanna call it." We still had not adequately defined our relationship.

Lukas seemed sincere. "Go for it," I said.

"Your dad seems to get after you a lot about grading and schoolwork all the time and about not having too much of a social life. And I've noticed that since

I've been here, you don't seem to go out a lot. Why is that?"

That was a difficult question to answer. I struggled to find the right words. "Well, taking care of you is a huge responsibility. I take that responsibility very seriously," I began.

Lukas clearly didn't buy it. "That might be true now that I'm here, but not before." He flicked his brush in my direction, covering me with spots of paint. "Dude, you gotta learn to have some fun. Now, let's hear the real story," he added.

It might be easier for me to just tell him why I became a teacher. I put my paintbrush down and sat on the edge of his bed, next to a monstrous pile of clothes that desperately needed to be washed. The smell almost made me pass out.

"You never met my mom, did you?" I asked. He might have seen pictures of her.

"No, I never met her. I heard she died before I was born."

"She did. Did you know she was also a teacher?" I continued. Lukas seemed surprised to find out that there was another teacher in the family.

My mom had taught history for years at Encino High School. She was unbelievably dedicated to her students. This was a time before enforced student/ teacher boundaries, and it was not uncommon for students to meet teachers over coffee to hash out their personal problems. My mom worked diligently to make sure that each and every one of her students got the attention he or she deserved. It was a tireless effort that lacked immediate gratification. (That part was still true today.)

One night, when I was a freshman in high school, Mom picked me up from a Science Olympiad practice. As we returned home along Ventura Boulevard, her pager went off. One of her students had forgotten her textbook and study guide at school; the student needed at least one of them to prepare for a big test the following day.

I looked at my mom. "She's paging you *now*?"

"Do you mind if we turn around?" she asked. "I can at least give her a copy of the study guide." Her commitment always shone through. That was the kind of teacher she was. Who was I to argue?

Mom turned the car around and headed back up Ventura Boulevard toward Woodland Hills. We pulled into the Ralph's parking lot and she got out. I sat in the front seat and fiddled with the car stereo as she ran across the street to meet her student.

I saw my mom hand over the packet of class notes and have a short conversation with her student before giving her a hug. Then she turned to cross back over Ventura Boulevard.

She never made it back to the car.

Lukas' eyes were wide. "She..."

"Yes." I paused a moment. "Now you know why I decided to let you stay with me."

"Why's that?" Lukas had a talent for asking probing, difficult questions.

"Teaching is all about giving students opportunities," I said. "You needed help and I knew I had to give you that help." I hoped that answer would suffice.

"So *that's* why you let me stay out here."

I smirked. "That, and I was tired of having no one to talk about at the lunch table. All they do is talk about is their kids." That was very true.

"So now I'm a charity case." Lukas flung a second batch of paint my way, but missed.

"I think when your mom asked me to do it, part of me knew it would be good for me and good for you," I said.

"Then, dude, you gotta promise me one thing."

"What's that?"

"You talk about being a writer, but I've never seen you work on your script. Get off your butt and get moving with it."

"That I can do," I said, smiling. For once, I thought I just might.

"Do it for yourself. And do it for me. Deal?" Lukas reached out his hand for a handshake. I quickly picked up my paintbrush and stuck it in his hand, and shook.

"You're an ass." Lukas deftly snapped a picture of his now ocean blue hand.

"I learned from the best," I replied. Another volley of ocean blue paint came in my direction.

TEN

Spring had arrived in southern California, and Lukas was very excited about the prospect of trying out for the Malibu High spring soccer team. He sat at the kitchen table one morning before school with a sheepish grin on his face. An official school form sat next to him. Lukas was very good about dancing around an issue before he got to the main point. I figured I'd pre-empt the whole routine.

"Hey, morning," he began. "I wanted..."

"... to ask me for what?" I finished.

"How did you know I was going to ask you for something?"

By now we'd lived together long enough that I knew his little quirks as well as he knew mine. Lukas forgot that I had worked with kids long enough to know every trick in the book.

"So, I was thinking about trying out for spring soccer."

"Well that sounds like it would be fun."

"I haven't played since the fall and my skills are starting to wane."

"Starting to wane? Really?" *What kid uses the word 'wane'?* I thought.

"OK, I'm getting rusty. Are you ok with me signing up? Can you sign the form?" He slid the form over to me.

I looked it over. "You seem to have missed something in your request," I said dryly.

"What's that?"

"Your hand's not out for the $500 fee."

"I thought you'd be willing to spot me that." There was the financial request.

"I'm thinking not."

Lukas looked shocked. "What do you mean, 'I'm thinking not'?"

"Five hundred is a lot of money. I think maybe you could get a job to earn that."

"Dude, are you serious? You want me to work?"

"Sure. If I want something, I work for it. If you want something, you can work for it too."

TOPANGA CANYON BLVD

Lukas pounded the pavement for a week before he found a job at the Topanga Market as a bagboy. That lasted two days before he realized he couldn't fill patrons' reusable bags in an organized way. That, and he spent too much time socializing in the staff breakroom.

After another search, Lukas finally got a job as a busboy at Malibu Coffee + Tea. The pay was minimum wage and the hours were limited, and it would probably have taken him until he graduated to make the necessary $500 soccer team registration fee. I gave him the money under the condition that he pay me back. Lukas seemed determined to meet this financial obligation.

I had promised him that I wouldn't stop by MC+T when he was working. However, one afternoon, I had left school late and the line at the local Starbucks was too long. I thought it was safe to go there. I was wrong.

I walked in and was surprised to see Lukas behind the counter, trying to figure out how to use the espresso machine. He looked frazzled. The place was filled with restless customers waiting to be served.

He spotted me in line. "Hey, you said you wouldn't come in when I was working," he called out. "I don't want you weirding me out."

"I didn't know you were working today," I replied. That was true.

"I got called in. Someone else called out."

"And why are you behind the counter?" I didn't know he could even make coffee. Considering all the trouble he was having with the espresso machine, I'm not sure advanced coffee-making was in his skill set.

He said that his boss had wanted him to cover the counter for "just a minute." That was five minutes ago. Lukas was surprised when an old ladies' bridge club showed up. He'd done his best to stall them but they were getting annoyed and complaining in increasingly loud voices.

"Do you want me to give you a hand?" It was the least I could do.

"Some advice would help. I'm just supposed to be a bus boy bussing."

I stayed on the customer side of the counter. Several of the old ladies approached, having noticed our interaction. "This young lad seems to be not making our coffee," one of them complained.

I challenged the ringleader. "The young lad is new. Let him take your order again and he'll get things moving. Don't you remember your first day on the job?" *It was probably as Adam and Eve's nanny*, I thought.

The leader rattled off a list of fifteen highly complex coffee orders. Lukas wrote them down feverishly.

"Now double check the order with the woman," I whispered in Lukas' ear. He'd gotten all the orders right.

I spied Lukas' manager coming from the bathroom area, and ducked around the corner.

The manager apologized to Lukas for taking so long. As he got back to work, he complimented Lukas on a fine job taking the orders and stalling the customers long enough for him to return.

Lukas passed me a free hot coffee and smiled. He mouthed *thanks*. I was one lucky dad.

Lukas had managed to balance his soccer practice, soccer games, schoolwork, and job. His grades had suffered a bit, but he kept his nose to the grindstone, as my dad would say. I'd actually never seen anyone do that—nor had I ever seen a grindstone.

Mondays were always late days for me. There was usually a faculty meeting or department meeting after school. I often struggled with getting home in time to make dinner, but since Lukas' voracious appetite meant he ate non-stop all day, I didn't worry about it too much. I was still amazed that, with his significant caloric intake, he still remained razor thin.

Tonight, he was sprawled out on the sofa, watching TV. He would randomly take a piece of popcorn, toss it in air, aiming for his mouth. The area around the sofa was littered with popcorn.

I looked at the TV. "What *are* you watching?" I asked.

"A repeat of *Saved by the Bell*." Apparently, he had developed a new affinity for '80s sitcoms. "It's the one where Jessie becomes addicted to caffeine pills." I was ashamed to admit I'd seen it—many times.

"I thought you had soccer practice this afternoon," I said, looking on.

"It was cancelled. And why are *you* so late?"

"Our faculty meeting ran over." I really hated those meetings.

There was a pause. "I'm hungry," he said finally, without looking away from the screen.

"What do you want for dinner?" I asked. "We can go out. I can make something. Whatever you want."

Lukas remained glued to the TV set. He seemed entranced by Jessie's "I'm so excited" outburst. "Huh?" was all he could muster as a response.

I loudly repeated the request. "*What do you want for dinner?*"

Lukas jabbed his thumb in the direction of the kitchen. I looked over and saw that the dining room table had already been set. A large bowl of spaghetti sat in the middle of the table next to a small bowl of meatballs.

"What … is this?" I asked.

"I decided to make dinner for you."

I walked over to the table and took a deep breath. The spaghetti smelled good. Then I spied the DoorDash receipt tucked under the napkin.

"Make dinner … or order it?"

Lukas leapt over the sofa and smiled. "OK, so I ordered it, dude. I knew you'd be hungry by the time you got home."

"Well, it's very thoughtful of you." I gave him a hug. He snapped a picture of the food and seemed pleased with himself.

Lukas typically stared down at his food and then shoveled it in his mouth. Tonight, he was much more talkative. That usually meant he wanted something, but he was just chatty. I asked him how his classes were going. The end of the semester was getting close and I was pleased that I hadn't received any "academic updates" yet.

"I think I'm doing pretty good."

"That's a rather generic interpretation."

"Am I getting all A's? No. But no C's."

"How about chemistry?"

"That's my best class. It's awesome. Even if we don't get to blow things up." He imitated an explosion going off with his hands once again, before returning to his food and cleaning his plate. With all of his talking, I was amazed he could finish the spaghetti. With all of my active listening, I had barely touched mine.

"What's the matter?" he said, noticing this. "Don't you like it?"

I stopped and looked at him for a minute. Six months ago, I couldn't imagine a life with Lukas. Now I couldn't imagine a life without him.

"No, it's really good," I said at last. *What a lame comment*, I thought.

Lukas pulled out a bag out from under the table. "I have something else for you."

I looked at the bag and then at Lukas. "What's this?"

"You've treated me really well the last couple of months. Better than anyone has treated me—or should treat me."

I pulled a new laptop out of the bag with shock. "You didn't steal this, did you?"

Lukas flung a forkful of spaghetti in my direction. "No. I bought it. Legit."

"But how—and why?"

"I thought you might need a new laptop to work on your script," he said.

"But how did you afford it?"

"I worked a few extra shifts, skipped a few soccer practices."

"Is that why you aren't at practice today?" I asked.

He admitted that he'd been suspended from the team for missing too many practices. I wasn't happy that he'd been suspended but I appreciated the effort. I figured I'd talk to his coach and try to get him back on the team.

"Like I said, you've been so good to me. It was time I returned the favor."

I felt a tear well up in my eye.

ELEVEN

Two weeks later, I was still amazed at how well Lukas had motivated me to get back to work on my script. I'd wake up early to work on it before school and stay up after Lukas went to bed to continue my work. I wasn't convinced my writing was very good, but I felt like I had a compelling story that I wanted to tell. I also signed up for a television writing class at UCLA, my alma mater. Lukas called me "college dude." He'd have to start thinking about his own college plans soon enough.

One afternoon, I dropped Lukas off at his job on the way to my first class. "What time are you working to?" I asked. I hated ending sentences in prepositions.

"9. I think." Lukas had woeful time management skills. He'd probably figure out that his shift was over when someone turned the lights out. He told me he'd get a ride home from Emery and promised to be home by 9:15 before heading into work.

The traffic along the PCH and Sunset Boulevard was woefully slow. I was eager to get to class early and "reserve" a seat right by the windows, establishing it as mine for the semester. Ever since I was in high school, I always liked sitting either at the end of a row or near the windows. That meant one less person I'd have to talk to.

It had been ten years since I last stepped onto the UCLA campus. Maybe it was because I was a teacher, or maybe it was because I was excited by the pursuit of new knowledge, but either way, the college environment was still intoxicating to me. I knew every building here was brimming with scholars debating old theories and proposing new ideas. I loved to learn. That was the nerdy part of me.

I found my classroom in Kaplan Hall and quickly found a seat at the end of the second row. As class time approached, the room slowly filled with fresh-faced students who were all significantly younger than me and had invariably been out late partying the night before. I immediately felt out of place and started to sweat.

A woman of about forty entered. I assumed that she was the professor, but she turned out to be a student. She sat next to me, leaving the required buffer seat between us, and introduced herself as Lorelei, an aspiring TV writer from Glendale. Lorelei had a similar story to mine: her daughter had encouraged her to take the class so that Lorelei could finally write the great American television show. My nerves over being the oldest student in the room finally waned. Lukas had successfully motivated me to take the class, and now I felt like I had made a new friend.

Just a couple hours later, I left class, my mind abuzz with loglines, possible characters, and episode ideas. When I pulled into the driveway, I noticed that the lights were out. It was 9:30 PM and Lukas should have been home by now. I took his backpack and my briefcase from the car and headed in, dropping them by the sofa once I got inside.

"Lukas? Are you home?" I called out. No loud music. No response. I wondered where he was. I checked my phone—no messages.

I sat down on the sofa, pulled out my laptop, and checked my email. I looked down at Lukas' backpack and saw his last chemistry test sticking out of the top. I couldn't resist looking at it, and was pleased to see he had scored a 92. Behind that was an English paper on *Hamlet*. The paper was covered with red ink, with the words "See me" written at the top—words that strike fear into the heart of every student. British Literature had been the lowest grade on his report card, and it appeared that he was still struggling with his writing.

By now it was 11 PM. I turned off the lights and sat in solitary darkness, reflecting on how much my life had changed over the past few months since Lukas arrived.

I soon heard the familiar crunch of feet on driveway pebbles outside, and knew Lukas was home. Then I heard him climb onto the deck. Apparently, he didn't want to come in through the front door. He saw that the sliding door was open, and pushed it a little bit further before entering.

My timing had to be perfect. Just as he closed the door and turned around, I snapped a picture. The flash from my phone surprised and scared him, and he froze in place.

"Can I help you?" I asked. I thought I'd have some fun with this.

"I can explain," he said immediately. I'm sure his mind was whirring like crazy, trying to come up with a believable story. This was going to be good.

"Let's hear it."

Lukas explained that Emery had met him promptly at 9. Emery's dad had been giving him a hard time about his potential recruitment to a Division I school, and was always pushing him to meet with swimming coaches. Emery found the whole process frustrating and "just needed to talk." He had been there for Lukas many times, and Lukas thought it was appropriate to return the favor.

Lukas plopped down onto the sofa. "We talked for a little bit on the beach. I know I should have called. I'm sorry I'm late." He sighed and tensed up, awaiting punishment.

I found it was easier to just let him off the hook. "That's ok. Just make sure you call next time." Then I pulled his *Hamlet* paper out and asked him what happened. He seemed surprised that we were going to talk about academics at 11 PM, but he didn't accuse of me of going through his backpack.

"Do you always have your teacher hat on?" he asked.

"I didn't have it on two minutes ago."

Lukas assured me that he had met with his Brit Lit teacher, who had given him a lot of advice about how to improve both his writing and analysis. Lukas admitted that he struggled with reading comprehension and getting his ideas on paper. We had similar challenges: I had trouble actually sitting down and getting my ideas for a TV show on paper, too.

"I get to do a rewrite," he said. "I just need to have it in by Friday." Lukas promised me he'd have it done by then.

"Do you want me to ground you for breaking curfew and make you stay in to finish it?" I was uncertain how to act. I felt like Monty Hall on *Let's Make a Deal*.

"Or do you want to trust that I'll show it to you before I turn it in?" Lukas countered. He also knew how to make a deal. I could tell by the sincerity in his voice that he'd get it done well—and on time—and I agreed to his terms.

Lukas smiled and headed up to bed. I looked at his beaten-up black Converse sneakers on the floor. "Yep, this is turning out to be ok," I said to myself.

TWELVE

I knew how much being on the soccer team meant to Lukas, so I worked a little magic with the soccer coach to get him back on the team. But it cost me. I didn't have to sign my life away—just agree to tutor his daughter for her upcoming calculus final. I knew what it was like to have a kid who sometimes struggled academically.

Lukas' final game of the season was today, and while the team wouldn't be heading to any championships, I wanted to be there to support him. I'd been at every one of his games this season. During each game, Lukas would always look toward the sidelines, checking for my attendance. I knew how much it meant to him to have me there. He had told me once that his parents never attended his soccer games in Miami.

It was strange for me to be on the sidelines during the game. The parents in attendance saw me as a teacher supporting his students. I tried explaining that Lukas was my cousin, but by the time I got to the end of the story, they were either confused or had lost interest in what I was saying. I often found myself standing alone on the sidelines while the parents stood together in a group, sipping coffee or noshing on organic scones.

TOPANGA CANYON BLVD

Lukas arrived at the soccer field early to practice his goaltending. He was running through his regular series of pre-game warm ups when Emery approached him.

"Dude, big game today," Lukas said by way of greeting. It was the final game of the season, and he wanted to go out on a win.

Emery had been at every game all season as well, and knew the team would miss Lukas' presence and leadership when he headed back to Miami. Lukas had really elevated their level of play.

"I hope there are no nutmegs today," he said, trying to sound like he knew a lot about soccer. He had failed.

Lukas laughed. "What are you, dude, some type of ESPN commentator? You're a swimmer."

Emery grew serious. "Dude, I'm going to miss you when you head back to Miami."

"Now don't go and get all sentimental," Lukas said.

"We've shared a lot since you've been here," Emery said.

Lukas smiled. Over this short time, he and Emery had become best friends. "We have," he agreed. "I can't tell you how much it means to me."

Other team members had arrived by now and started their pre-game warm ups as well. Lukas looked around to see if I had arrived yet. He was a little dejected when he didn't see me on the sidelines.

"Text Noah and remind him about the game," he said to Emery, worried.

I was in my office, neatly placing folders in my briefcase. My phone chirped with a text from Emery, reminding me about Lukas' final soccer game. I was just about to leave the office when the phone rang. I hesitated to answer, but since it was coming from the main office, I knew I couldn't ignore it. At the other end of the line, Cynthia told me that there was to be an emergency student meeting in a few minutes.

"But I have to get to Lukas' soccer game. It's just about to start," I said. I knew it was hopeless. No one ever got out of emergency student meetings.

Cynthia promised me that it would be quick. *Famous last words*, I thought. I scooped up my briefcase and ran to the office.

As the soccer game started, Lukas looked to the sidelines again and did not see me. He did find Emery in the crowd and, while the action was at the other end of the field, drew a big question mark in the air. Emery looked around to see if he could find me and just shrugged his shoulders. Lukas was disappointed.

Just before the end of the first half, Lukas blocked a tough shot to keep the Malibu team comfortably ahead by a score of 3 to 1.

TOPANGA CANYON BLVD

Meanwhile, I sat at the corner of the conference table in Principal Williams' office as the faculty discussed the academic challenges faced by one of the juniors. We had to go around the table and give a brief assessment of this student's strengths and areas of growth. Some teachers were short and to the point. Others felt it necessary to drone on and on about some minor detail. This was not going to be a short meeting. I looked at my watch and realized I had missed most of the first half.

As the meeting continued, Principal Williams noticed that I kept looking at my watch. "Do you have someplace else you'd rather be?" he asked severely.

"My apologies. Lukas is playing in his last soccer game this afternoon. I haven't missed a game all season."

"You have anything else you'd like to contribute?"

"No sir." I didn't even have this kid as a student.

"Then get out of here." I grabbed my briefcase and ran to the soccer field.

Lukas planted himself in the goal box as the soccer teams took to the field for the second half. The opposing team's forward was a talented player who lived for the challenge of outfoxing the other team's goalie. In one quick shot early in the half, the attacker kicked the ball toward the corner of the goal. Lukas reacted as quickly as he could, leaping to block the ball. But he wasn't able to stop soon enough. Banging the side of his body into the goalpost, he fell to the ground, screaming an obscenity.

Immediately, the whole team rushed over to him. The coach went through a quick concussion protocol before asking Lukas if he felt like he had broken something. Lukas said he felt ok, just in pain—real pain. The team trainer helped Lukas stand up and escorted him off the field, where he sat in agony on the bench.

As that moment, I arrived at the game, and was surprised to see the opposing team lingering on the field. The Malibu team was gathered around the bench. I asked one of the organic scone parents what was going on.

"The goalie collided with the goalpost," he said. My heart stopped. That would be Lukas.

I pushed my way through the team to find Lukas sitting on the bench, an ice pack on his arm. He was grimacing in pain.

"Are you ok?" I figured I'd start with a simple question, as opposed to explaining why I was late.

"Nice of you to show up." There wasn't even a *dude* at the end.

"I'm sorry I'm late," I said. "I got stuck in a meeting." I was trying to justify my absence. It wasn't working.

"So, a meeting is more important than watching me play?" Lukas snapped back. The team grew restless and started to disperse and return to the field.

"All I can say is I'm sorry," I said simply.

Lukas started crying. "You know, you're just like everyone else. You put me last." I was dumbfounded, and he continued. "If I wanted to be ignored, I could have just stayed in Miami."

"That's not fair and you know it," I said. I'd been with him every step of the way.

Then he unloaded years' worth of anger and frustration on me. "You know what's not fair?" he asked, his face twisted with anger. "People telling me they care when they really don't." For the final insult, he added, "Get lost."

He needed space. I took a deep breath and stood up. "I'll see you at home," I said.

Lukas flew into a rage as I turned and left. "Right. Walk away, just like everyone else." For the first time since he had arrived, I had really disappointed him. I'd disappointed myself as well.

Emery came up to me. "He doesn't mean it, Mr. Whitmore. He's just in pain."

"Make sure he gets home," I said. I sighed. "I doubt he wants a ride home from me."

"I will, Mr. Whitmore. I will. You have my word."

I drove down the PCH, devastated. It was painful to have Lukas unload on me like that, especially in public. I actually started crying, and pulled off into Will Rogers State Beach to park the car. The benches here were notoriously hard and the one I had sat on was certainly no different. I sat still and stared out over the ocean, trying to calm down.

The beach had been recently swept, but the smoothness of the sand was disturbed by two separate sets of footprints, that joined to form one unified set of prints headed toward the ocean. *What a metaphor*, I thought. I picked up my phone and took a picture.

Just then, there was a tap on my shoulder. I looked up to see Pat standing behind me.

"What are you doing here?" I asked, startled. I was embarrassed that she had found me sitting there alone.

"Emery told me what happened at the game," she said. "I saw you drive off and followed you here." She sat down on the bench next to me. "Wanna talk?"

There really wasn't much to say. I sat in silence. I often struggled with sharing my feelings, even with a close friend or colleague. I found it embarrassing.

"You know he's been coming to talk to me. Once a week," she said. That surprised me.

"Do you really think he hates me?" I asked helplessly. I was hoping the answer was no.

"No, he doesn't. By the way, he gave me permission to talk to you about it, if it ever came to that."

"What has he said?" I was curious.

"It's better coming from him," she said. "But I can tell you this. It was only a matter of time before he exploded."

"So, maybe I didn't do anything wrong?" I asked hopefully. I was looking for leniency.

"In his mind, you did." She paused and considered her next words. "I'm not sure you realize how much he appreciates you." Pat saw that I was overwhelmed and quickly changed the subject.

Pat handed me an envelope. "This was dropped off right after you left," she said, getting up to leave. "Now go find Lukas."

Lukas sat on the bench at the Top of Topanga, a small park and picnic area that overlooked the San Fernando Valley. The benches here were notoriously hard and the one he had sat on was certainly no different. He sat still and stared out over the valley, trying to calm down.

He was still in his soccer kit and couldn't stop crying. He'd taken out a lifetime of frustrations on me, just because I'd been late to one soccer game. He felt awful about it, knowing everything I had done for him in the past few months.

Just then, he felt a tap on his shoulder. He looked up and saw Emery standing behind him. "How did you find me?" Lukas asked.

"Mr. Whitmore told me to go after you. I saw you grab your gear and hop in that Uber."

Lukas nodded and kept crying. Emery stood there awkwardly for a moment. "Why'd you come here?" he asked at last.

"I heard it's a good place to reflect."

"Do you want me to leave you alone?" Emery replied, wanting to respect his friend's wishes.

"No." Lukas wanted him to stay. He sighed. "How could I do that to him?" he asked, trying to understand his own behavior.

"Dude, you didn't mean it. You were in pain."

"Did you see the look on his face? I thought *he* was going to start crying." Lukas was disappointed in himself. How could he have been so cruel? "I'm probably gonna be sent back to Florida on the next flight," he moaned.

"He's not going to do that. You just need to talk to him," Emery assured him. He took a step back. "I'm going to sit in my car. You let me know when you're ready to go."

As Emery walked away, Lukas squeezed his body into a ball and rocked back and forth on the bench. Tears flooded from his eyes. Regardless of what Emery had said, he felt like he'd blown the best family relationship he'd ever had.

Just then, Lukas' phone chirped. It was a text: "Meet me at the Canyon Diner, if you wish. My treat."

Lukas started crying again.

I pulled into the parking lot of the Canyon Diner. It was unusually busy. Olivia greeted me at the door. "Where's the kid?"

"He's supposed to be meeting me here."

"You know, you two are the cutest. I mean in a father-son kind of way."

I mumbled thanks. I didn't know if Lukas would show. He could be anywhere right now. I could only hope that Emery had found him.

At our usual table under the bug zapper, I sat quietly, sipping my water and looking around at the other tables. At some, star-crossed lovers were having their first, second or tenth date. At others, large families squabbled over who would take the last piece of bread. My life had come full circle. I was alone again. I felt like the eyes of every patron in the place were on me. I decided to leave.

I got up and pushed my chair in. Just then, someone tapped me on my shoulder.

"Going somewhere, mister?" I turned around. It was Lukas.

Relief flooded me. "What are you doing here?" I asked.

"Well, you texted me to meet you here, so here I am." He gave me a big hug that was followed by a loud "oww."

"You still in pain?" I decided to show some of the parental concern I failed to demonstrate before.

"Physically, yes. Emotionally, not so much."

"Are you hungry?" He always was.

"Dude, I'm famished." We sat down at the table. Olivia approached.

"Well, look who's here. Hey, sweetness."

Lukas smirked.

"You guys want the usual?" she asked. Lukas was ready for a hefty serving of spaghetti and meatballs. That was too many carbs for me. I stuck with the fish and chips.

After Olivia took our orders and walked away, I looked at Lukas. "Who's going to go first?"

Lukas wiped his eyes. I could tell he'd been crying. "I'm so sorry, dude. You've been there so much for me and I treated you really bad."

"Badly," I said automatically.

"Do you always have to be a teacher? Can't you just be a dad?"

It had taken me a while to balance the two. I promised Lukas I'd do better.

Lukas told me about his sessions with Dr. Branigan and his struggle with isolation and loneliness. He was deeply concerned that I was lonely too. That's why he pushed me so hard to get back into my writing. But he'd also admitted that he could never fully express how much the last few months had meant to him.

I felt like a huge weight had been lifted off my shoulders as well. My parenting might not have been perfect, but it had been effective. I told Lukas I'd do my best to be the best cousin-as-dad I could be before he left.

He smiled and said, "Wanna shake on it, dude?" The *dude* was back. I knew things would be all right.

"Deal," I said.

"No paintbrushes this time, right?" As Olivia returned with our food, Lukas took out his phone and asked her to take a photo to memorialize the day.

We finished dinner. As I stood up, the envelope that Pat gave me fell out of my pocket.

"Dude, what's that?" Lukas asked.

"Oh, Dr. Branigan gave it to me before."

"Looks official. Open it, open it."

I started to open it, being careful not to rip the letter inside. Lukas reached out and grabbed it. "Dude, you are way too slow."

Lukas pulled the letter from the envelope and read it. His jaw dropped.

"Dude, you've been named Teacher of the Year!"

Thirteen

A week later, I was still amazed I'd been named Teacher of the Year. The nomination process was secretive: any teacher, student, or administrator could nominate any other teacher, student, or administrator for their respective award. This was an award not to be taken lightly. While I'd only receive a plaque and a check for $500 (that would somehow end up in Lukas' pocket), it was public recognition of all of my hard work and dedication over the past ten years at Malibu High.

The day before the awards ceremony, I took Lukas to Westfield Topanga to buy him a suit. If he could have worn a T-shirt and shorts to the ceremony, he would have. He was not a Men's Wearhouse suit kind of guy. Still, he knew this was a special moment for me and he wanted to "look sharp," as he said. After working our way through Macy's, JC Penney and about five stores that specialized in young men's attire, we found ourselves in the Hugo Boss store. I reminded Lukas that the prices here would break the budget of the average teacher. He reminded me I'd won $500.

A young woman in a tight dress came over to help us. Her nametag read "Pancake." I wondered if her sister's name was Waffle.

"I need a suit," Lukas announced loudly. Pancake asked what size suit jacket Lukas wore.

"I don't know. Like my size?"

I rolled my eyes. I told Pancake that Lukas was often a wiseass. She suggested he was cute. Great—a twenty-five-year-old woman named Pancake flirting with a high school boy.

Pancake pulled a black checkered suit from the rack and gave it to Lukas. "Sweet. Can I get it, dude?" he asked. Clearly, Lukas did not understand the art of trying on clothes before buying.

After a few minutes in the dressing room, he stepped back out for my opinion. It was a perfect fit. Even his black Converse sneakers looked good with the suit.

Pancake said that the suit looked hot on Lukas. He blushed. Turning to me, he asked, "Can I get it?" Then he looked at the price tag. "It's only $695."

I gasped, my shock causing me to slip into British lingo. "That's more than the bloody award. Are you daft?" There was sure to be a financial literacy seminar for Lukas in the near future.

Lukas pulled his usual puppy dog "can I have it?" face. I fell for it every time.

"Ok, we'll take it," I said. Honestly, I didn't have the energy to continue suit shopping.

Lukas bounced back into the dressing room to change, and Pancake smiled. "Nice kid you got there."

"He's my cousin. It's complicated."

By the time we left Hugo Boss, Lukas was famished, as he subtly indicated by rubbing his stomach. We headed to Massis Kabob, his favorite place to eat at the mall. Not only was the food good, but Lukas liked the fact that it was "The Original Kabobery." Lukas thought the word "kabobery" was funny. I wondered if there were unoriginal kaboberies out there.

We placed our orders and pushed our trays down the counter. When we got to the register, Lukas pulled out his wallet. "My treat," he said.

I laughed. Even though the Hugo Boss suit had broken the bank, I told Lukas he didn't have to pay.

"I'm only here for another month," he said, insisting. "It's the least I can do."

We picked up our food and found a table in the food court, surrounded by people speaking in more languages than at a UN General Assembly meeting. Talk about diversity!

Lukas smiled. "Do you think I can come visit you over the summer?" he asked. "Emery invited me to go up to his family cabin in Big Bear."

I could only smile in response. "I'd thought about renting out your room. But you'll do for a part-time summer resident."

Lukas stopped eating and grew serious. "Do you regret doing this?" he asked.

"Having lunch at Massis Kabob? No! The food here is good."

"No, dude. Taking me in for the semester."

I had to be honest. "It's one of the best things I've ever done. I'd do it all over again if I could. Heck, I'd let you stay if you wanted to."

"Really?" Lukas asked in disbelief.

"Sure. I like having you here."

"Cuz I was gonna ask if I could stay through the summer," he added.

I dropped my fork. It hit a piece of beef and sent it flying towards a table of teenagers next to us. Lukas laughed. "Always doing physics, aren't you?"

Lukas' question had surprised me. I think even he was surprised he had asked it, but he persisted. "Dude, would you let me stay?"

I would, but that was not my decision to make. That decision belonged to Miles and Lisa.

I told Lukas I would think about it.

The night of the awards ceremony had finally arrived. I sat nervously in the living room, wearing the suit I had bought, on sale and with a coupon, from the Kohl's Collection. I'd just gotten off the phone with Lisa when Lukas came bouncing down the stairs. The $695 Hugo Boss suit looked good on him. He'd paired it with a plain white T-shirt and—you guessed it—black Converse sneakers.

"Handsome enough for you?" he asked, seeking approval for his sartorial choices.

I knew if I said no, I'd have blown $700. All I said was, "You look good."

"Thanks. You look good too." Lukas looked at his watch. "What time do we have to be there?"

"Oh, like ten minutes ago. Maybe if you didn't spend so much time in the bathroom..."

"Dude, this look does not come naturally. It takes time."

I told Lukas that his mom had called and she wanted him to call him back.

"Did she say what she wanted?"

"Nope. I think she just wanted to say hi. Apparently, you've been doing a poor job of communicating with your parents of late."

"I've been busy," Lukas called out as he headed for the door. "She can wait. This is more important. I'll call her when we get back."

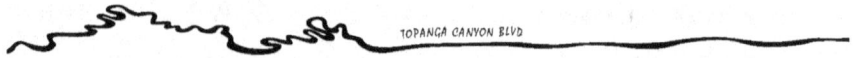

TOPANGA CANYON BLVD

This was a big event. Not exactly red carpet, but one of the biggest events at Malibu High.

I was seated in the front row with my dad and Lukas next to me. Pat and Emery were behind us. I started sweating.

The Student of the Year Award was given out first. Lukas muttered under his breath that he deserved that award more than the kid who'd built schools in Zimbabwe. The Administrator of the Year Award came next, and was given to someone who had been with the system for over fifty years. I thought that was a long time to wait for recognition.

Then Principal Williams called out my name as the recipient of the Teacher of the Year Award. Lukas whacked my back so hard that I thought I would fall out of my chair.

"Dude, that's you," he screamed in my ear.

Principal Williams read out a long list of my accomplishments as Lukas muttered under his breath, "dude, you do a lot." He then read my educational philosophy (never give up on a kid), and some biographical information from the nomination form, before calling me up.

I felt my phone vibrate in my suit pocket as I walked onstage, but ignored it for now. Principal Williams shook my hand, handed me the plaque (the check was direct deposit), and offered me the microphone. I was still sweating as I profusely thanked Principal Williams, all the administrators, every student I'd ever taught and every teacher I'd ever worked with. It was wordy, but effective.

Lukas was busy taking a picture. I looked directly at him as I said more. "Here's what I always tell my students—and myself. Dream big. Imagine positive and possible futures. Communicate hope. Know your why. Recognize what you can do. Be patient. And build trust."

A huge grin spread over Lukas' face as he listened. He knew that I was talking specifically about him. And he knew that I meant it.

Lukas stood up and pointed at me. "And that is my dad," he called out.

I smiled and pointed back at Lukas. "And that is the best kid ever."

FOURTEEN

Lukas and I sat together in the anteroom of the funeral home. His world had changed considerably over the past week.

"I should have called her back when I had the chance," he said at last.

"Yes, you probably should have," I said, gently.

Lukas started crying. "Isn't this where you tell me some mumbo jumbo about not regretting the decisions we make in life?" he asked through his tears.

I was not good with platitudes. "Do you really think that's gonna help?"

"Probably not," he agreed, glumly. "It's never helped before." He managed a weak smile.

I knew this had to be the most difficult day of his life.

"Hey, at least you're getting your money's worth for the suit." I never expected him to have to wear that Hugo Boss twice in a week.

Lukas frowned. "You know it was bound to happen," he said finally.

"Your mom dying?" It seemed like an odd thing to say.

"Not that. Well, yeah, we all die sometime." *That was direct*, I thought. "I meant me using up all of my good."

I was confused. "What's your good?"

Lukas explained that he believed that there was only a certain amount of good allotted to each person. When that good was used up, it was your turn for bad things. Once you had suffered through your allotment of bad, you had earned the same amount back in good. It was a binary argument that made no sense to me, but I could see how it would make sense to someone younger and more inexperienced.

I told Lukas that the world didn't work that way. Good things happen to good people and bad things happen to good people, and it wasn't a trade-off. There was enough good in the world to go around. Even if his idea was correct, I argued, he'd earned enough good over the past few months to keep him sustained for a while.

Lukas looked down at the floor. He'd actually worn dress shoes. I asked him if he wanted to be left alone for a while, or if he wanted to see his dad. The questions both earned a no in response.

The door to the anteroom opened and the funeral director told us that the service was about to begin.

"Are you ready?" I asked.

"Were you ready when you had to do this?"

"No one is ever ready," I conceded. I put my hand on Lukas' cheek and looked him directly in the eyes. "You can do this. You're Lukas Whitmore," I reminded him. Then I straightened his tie and gave him a hug.

"Dude, the suit. Watch the suit."

I laughed. He always had a way of breaking the tension with a sarcastic comment.

"Thanks, dad," he added.

I smiled. As he turned to head in, I said to myself, "Thanks, son."

He really was the best kid ever.

CREDITS

Photo p. 169 copyright © Eric A. Walters, 2018

Additional Credits

Photos p. 3 (et. al.) Shutterstock. Royalty-free stock photo ID 1198592200 with Shutterstock Enhanced License.

Topanga Map Designs by Imesami (fiverr.com)

Book Design by weformat (fiverr.com)

Book Cover Design by weformat (fiverr.com)

ABOUT THE AUTHOR

Eric Walters was born and raised in Massachusetts. He is a nationally-recognized science and technology educator and has authored several books and articles on innovative teaching and learning. He currently lives in New York City, and has a deep affinity for Southern California, especially In-N-Out Burger and Paramount Studios. *My Life With Lukas (On Topanga Canyon Boulevard): Best Kid Ever* is his third novel.

www.ingramcontent.com/pod-product-compliance
Lightning Source LLC
Chambersburg PA
CBHW071118100726
47908CB00008B/2415